AF426795

Loud Secrets

LOUD SECRETS

AKSHAYA SURESH

Preface

There are stories we tell the world, and then there are the ones we keep locked within ourselves, quiet, raw, and often too loud to silence. LOUD SECRETS was born from that very space within me. A space that longed to speak, not to impress, but to express.

This book is not fiction for the sake of entertainment. It's fiction layered with truth, my truth, your truth, and the quiet truth of countless others who carry invisible weight on their shoulders. It's a mirror held up to the parts of us that we often hide, the strength we downplay, and the struggles we never speak about.

I wrote LOUD SECRETS during the quietest hours of the day, when the world was asleep but my mind was wide awake. Every page carries the weight of thoughts I've battled with, beliefs I've held onto, and the fire that kept me going even when no one was watching.

This book isn't here to shout. It's here to resonate. To remind you that even if the world doesn't hear you, you can hear yourself, and that is more than enough.

If this book finds even one person who feels seen, understood, or empowered, then it has done exactly what it was meant to do.

Loud Secrets

Acknowledgment

LOUD SECRETS is not just a book, it's a voice I've held within for years. A dream that lived quietly in the corners of my mind, now finally brought to life through sleepless nights, early mornings, and unshakable willpower.

To my readers, thank you for choosing this journey. You didn't just pick up a book, you picked up a piece of me. I hope these pages remind you that even in silence, your strength speaks volumes. That nothing can stop you when your mind is made up.

To my Mom, when the world was busy teaching a woman to cook, you taught me to be independent! To my Dad who taught me to be brave. To my grandpa who is my backbone. To all my friends. To all my well-wishers who believed in me when even I did not! You've all been a silent strength in my every step.

To those who carry unspoken burdens yet show up every day with resilience, this book belongs to you. To the men who bear responsibilities with quiet grace, to the women who rise regardless of the weight on their shoulders, LOUD SECRETS echoes your courage.

And finally, to the version of me who wrote through exhaustion, trusted her thoughts, and refused to let go of her dream, you made it. This is your truth, shared with the world.

Loud Secrets

Your courage starts the moment you stop giving up!

Life is profoundly shaped by our perceptions of destiny, which can significantly impact the paths we take. Those who choose to embrace the journey, with all its ups and downs, often find themselves gaining valuable experiences that contribute to their personal and professional growth. In contrast, individuals who give up in the face of adversity miss out on these opportunities and may find themselves feeling unfulfilled as a result. Every bit and piece of circumstance that happens in life has a value.

Struggles and challenges are inevitable parts of any significant journey, whether it's in our career, relationship, or personal development. It's natural to feel exhausted when surrounded by obstacles. Resilience is the ability to bounce back from difficulties, and it is during these challenging times that we must dig deep and find the strength to move forward. As you charge ahead toward your next level of success, remember that destiny tends to reward those who face their fears and challenges with courage. It is often the person who perseveres and maintains their commitment to their objectives that ultimately achieves their dreams, while those who surrender to the pressures of life may remain stagnant.

Commit to be the best version of yourself in all aspects of your life. Focus on setting clear goals and take proactive steps toward achieving them. Surround yourself with supportive people who encourage your growth and share your vision. As you dedicate yourself to this journey, you will notice how destiny starts to align with your efforts, creating pathways to success that you might not have previously envisioned. With this approach, you will grow as a person and find that destiny can open doors for those willing to face life's challenges with courage and determination. learn from the mistakes, make sure you never repeat them, and wait for your magic destiny.

Your Strength lies in embracing who you are, despite the world's expectations!

To all the women, they say you are not allowed to

Not allowed to step out in a short dress.

Not allowed to travel, to explore.

Not allowed to make your own decisions.

Not allowed to love whom you choose.

Not allowed to speak up for your rights.

Not allowed to chase your dreams.

Not allowed to live without seeking permission.

And if you dare to break these unwritten rules, they will label you

Defiant. Stubborn. Reckless. Rebellious.

But tell me, aren't these names beautiful?

Aren't they the very essence of strength, courage, and freedom?

Stop feeling guilty for being exactly who you are.

It is okay to be obstinate when it comes to your dreams.

It is okay to stand firm in what you believe.

Yes, there will be consequences, but wouldn't you rather face them for a life you truly desire than waste away in a cage built by others?

Step out. Fly. Fall. Rise again.

Feel exhausted not from suppression, but from chasing what sets your soul on fire.

Walk your own path, not the one drawn for you.

And above all, remember this is your life. Live it your way.

Your Wisdom lies in adapting, not adopting!

Every individual is unique, and so is their perspective. Our views on life, situations, and challenges are shaped by our upbringing, experiences, and personal journey.

Expecting to adopt someone else's perspective entirely is neither practical nor beneficial. What works for them might align with their lifestyle, but it may not be suitable for ours.

Instead of blindly following another person's perspective, focus on gaining insights from their experiences. Learning from different viewpoints helps in making informed decisions, fostering growth, and broadening our understanding. However, true wisdom lies in analysing and adapting what resonates with our values rather than conforming without reflection.

At the same time, just as we value our perspectives, we must respect that others have their own. No one's perspective is universally right or wrong. Forcing our views onto someone else or dismissing theirs entirely only creates division. Growth comes from mutual understanding, considering different perspectives without imposing our own.

In the end, the goal is not to adopt or reject perspectives blindly but to learn, evolve, and make choices that align with our path while respecting the individuality of others.

Embrace life's lessons, even when they sting!

Lessons are always a wake-up call. They don't always come in a positive form, some are tough, painful, and even negative. But no matter how they arrive, they hold value.

The key is to process these lessons with your mind, not just your heart. The heart reacts emotionally, while the brain responds logically. By understanding this balance, we can apply our lessons effectively instead of letting them weigh us down.

Wake-up calls can come from different sources, people, experiences, stories, or even witnessing someone else's journey. What matters is how we receive them. Instead of feeling low when a wake-up call is difficult, take it wholeheartedly.

It isn't always about negativity; sometimes, even a compliment is a wake-up call. When someone acknowledges your strengths, it's a reminder that you have the potential to do more and be better.

Not everyone receives wake-up calls, and not everyone recognizes them when they do. But if someone truly believes in your potential and pushes you toward success, listen. Save those wake-up calls in your mind, implement the lessons, and use them as stepping stones. These moments are not setbacks, they are the biggest keys to your success.

Just celebrate your journey, not someone else's path!

There's a selfish giant inside all of us. It feeds on that uneasy feeling we get when someone else has what we do. Most people won't admit it, but it's there, hiding behind smiles and polite words.

Imagine finally getting something you've wanted for so long. You feel pure joy until you realize someone else has it too. Suddenly, that happiness feels smaller, as if it's been shared too many times to still be yours.

That's the secret no one talks about. The way comparison quietly steals our joy, the way we let it grow until it takes up space in our minds, making us forget what we already have. This selfish giant thrives in silence, feeding off our thoughts, and convincing us that our happiness isn't enough if someone else has the same.

But here's the loud truth: happiness doesn't shrink just because someone else feels it too. Success isn't any less meaningful just because another person reaches it as well. Life has a way of teaching us this, though we often realize it only when we look back.

So, how do you silence this giant? By refusing to compare. By choosing to own your journey, to celebrate your wins, no matter how small. Because when you truly appreciate what you have, that selfish giant fades, and in its place, real contentment takes root.

Pray with purpose, work with heart!

When you pray for something, you must also pay for it. But what should you pay? Pay with your love, your attention, your care, your time, pay with all your heart and soul. Only then can you turn prayers into reality.

A prayer alone is just a wish. Simply hoping or thinking, I have to do this or this will happen isn't enough. Nothing happens until you work for it. The difference between a dream and an achievement is action.

But here's the key: working for something you pray for should be soulful. It should not come with hesitation, regret, or resistance. Instead, it should be filled with love, care, and dedication. When you put your heart into something, it no longer feels like a burden; it becomes a part of who you are. Love what you do, and consistency will follow naturally.

Of course, maintaining consistency is easier said than done. As humans, we get distracted. Our minds get tired. And when that happens, staying committed becomes difficult. But if you truly want your prayers to be answered, you must keep working. To work, you must stay consistent.

Yes, your mind will get tired, but when it does, remind yourself of why you started. Think about the results that await you. Imagine holding the outcome of your prayers in your hands. That vision alone will push you forward, even when your energy fades.

So when you pray for something, don't just wait for it to happen. Work for it, stay consistent, and focus on the future that awaits you. That's how prayers turn into reality.

Love story doesn't need to be
perfect, being real matters!

There are days when love wraps you in comfort, making you feel safe and cherished, much like the sun that brings life and energy. On other days, love may feel like the gentle, cool glow of the moon, a soft light that guides you through moments of uncertainty, like an open sky that stretches beyond the limit

Yet, the beauty of love lies not in its perfection, but in its flow. True love is not measured by a rigid 50-50 balance; it can be 80-20, 10-90, or any ratio that feels right, as long as both people remain true to themselves. It is about embracing the authentic parts of who you are and allowing your relationship to grow organically, without trying to force it

The secret to a happy love life is simple: be yourself and let your partner be. Consider how the sky transforms with the passing of time. love, in all its forms, adds vibrancy to our lives. The joyful moments and the challenges alike weave together to create a rich tapestry of shared experiences.

In our ever-changing world, where expectations and comparisons can easily cloud our hearts, remember that your love story is uniquely yours. It is not about mimicking someone else's perfect tale or trying to maintain an impossible balance. It is about the honest, sometimes chaotic, and always beautiful process of two people coming together, supporting one another, and navigating life's twists and turns with courage and grace.

As you reflect on your journey of love, let the boundless sky be a constant reminder. Embrace every moment, the laughter, the tears, the victories, and the setbacks, as integral parts of a love

Even when battles are silent, they deserve to be seen!

A man's life is not just his own. From the moment he steps into the world, he carries the weight of responsibilities which is silent, unspoken, yet always present. As a boy, he is expected to be strong. As a student, he is told to think about his future. As a young man, he is pressured to build stability. As a husband, he must provide. As a father, he must protect. And in every stage, he is asked to be responsible, no matter what he truly wants. But who asks him how he feels?

He faces struggles he never speaks of. The days he breaks down but never shows. The nights he loses sleep worrying about his family's tomorrow. The moments he wishes to cry but holds back because the world has told him that men don't cry, men don't complain, men don't fall apart.

He walks through storms alone, shielding his loved ones from the harsh winds. He battles expectations, sacrifices his dreams, and makes choices not for himself, but for those who depend on him. Not all men are the same, but all men bear something heavy in their hearts, something they will never ask anyone to lighten.

And yet, despite it all, he stands tall.

Not because he has no pain, but because he refuses to let it define him. Not because he has no fears, but because he has people who trust in him. A man doesn't seek pity. He doesn't ask for applause. He just hopes that one day, someone will see his silent battles and say,

"You are valued. You are strong. And you deserve to live for yourself, too."

The rhythm is not in breaks, but in balance!

Sundays always bring a strange feeling, a mix of rest and uneasiness. The weekend is almost over, and the thought of Monday starts creeping in. We sigh, knowing that work, studies, or responsibilities are waiting for us again. It feels tiring even before it begins. But when Monday arrives, something changes. The moment we step into our routine, we start moving forward. The work that once felt heavy now gives us a sense of purpose. Maybe it's a small achievement, a task completed, or just the feeling of being productive. And in that moment, we realize, we deserve this.

As the days pass, the weight of the week starts building up. By Wednesday, exhaustion kicks in. The energy we had at the start begins to fade, and everything starts feeling repetitive. Waking up feels harder, motivation seems distant, and we wonder why every week feels the same. But the truth is, this tiredness is normal. It's not a sign that something is wrong. It just means we're moving forward.

Then comes Friday. The air feels lighter, the weight on our shoulders starts lifting, and the finish line is finally in sight. The same work that felt endless now feels like an achievement. We made it through the week, and that itself is a reason to be proud. The weekend's excitement fills us with relief, making all the struggles of the past days seem worth it.

And just like that, it's Sunday again. The cycle repeats. Some weeks feel harder than others, but in the end, every day has to be lived. There is no way to escape routine, no way to pause time. But maybe the goal was never to stop this cycle. Maybe the real secret is to stop fighting it. It's okay to feel exhausted, it's okay to feel frustrated. These feelings don't need to be fixed, because they are not problems. Instead of trying to make life perfect, just try to make it interesting. Find little moments of joy, no matter how small. After all, life is not about avoiding tiredness, but about finding reasons that make every day worth it.

Quiet work creates the loudest impacts!

In life, you will meet people who focus more on proving themselves right rather than genuinely growing. They don't necessarily bring others down, but they ensure that only their strengths are noticed. They project themselves in a way that overshadows the hard work of those around them. But here's the truth: No one can take away the effort you've put in. No one can erase the dedication, the sleepless nights, and the determination that went into your work. Success isn't about who claims credit the fastest, it's about who truly earns it.

If your efforts aren't being recognized today, don't let that shake your confidence. The universe has its way of rewarding those who persist with sincerity and passion. Your work will be seen, your talent will be acknowledged, and your time will come. It may not happen immediately, but it will be undeniable when it does.

When you genuinely feel happy for what you have, that is contentment. But when you start feeling bad because someone else also has what you have, or even more, you begin walking down a dangerous path. Success isn't about competing with others; it's about growing alongside them. If someone else is advancing in their life or career and you feel threatened instead of inspired, then you're not moving forward; you're holding yourself back. Growth is about becoming better than you were yesterday, not about resenting someone else's progress.

Let others focus on appearances if they want, you focus on real progress. Because in the long run, it's not about proving yourself to anyone. It's about becoming the best version of yourself, and that will always lead to true success.

Your hard work will shine at the right time, in front of the right people. Trust the process. Keep going. Nothing can stop you.

The moments you have right now
is a gift someone else prayed for!

Life is never truly fair. It challenges everyone in different ways, some face struggles with resilience, some silently endure, and others, overwhelmed by pain, make choices they never should. When hardships keep piling up, it feels like the world has singled out certain people for suffering while granting others an easy path. But the truth is, that problems are universal. What truly matters is how we face them.

Many people break under pressure when they feel alone. Support is not about solving someone's problems; it is about standing beside them as they fight their battles. Having even one person to lean on can mean the difference between pushing forward and giving up. Yet, not everyone has that. Those who lack support often fall into despair, believing there is no way out. That is why kindness, understanding, and just being there for someone can change everything.

In moments of darkness, it helps to step back and see life for what it is a gift. Many people in this world struggle without even the basic necessities: food, shelter, love. If we have these, we already have more than millions who wake up each day fighting just to survive. When problems consume us, we forget that simply existing is a privilege. Every breath we take is something someone else wished for. None of us chose to be born, but that does not give us the right to choose when we leave. Life was given to us without our permission, and one day, it will naturally be taken from us. That is how it is meant to be through the laws of nature, not by our own hands. No matter how unbearable life seems, no matter how relentless the struggles become, ending it is never the answer.

Every challenge is a battle, but each battle survived proves our strength. The pain we feel today is not permanent ,it is just a moment in time. And as long as we hold on, there will always be another chance for better days.

You are character is the only thing that endures!

Life teaches in the harshest ways. The lessons are brutal, and the truth is often unbearable. But one of the most unsettling realities is this ,people change. Not always for growth, not always for wisdom, but mostly for survival. Self-preservation has become the new morality. When trouble knocks, people don't just react ,they transform. They abandon loyalty, discard principles, and rewrite their character in seconds. And the worst part? They don't even flinch while doing it.

They will hurt you if it means saving themselves. They will pretend you don't exist if it benefits their reputation. They will switch sides without hesitation, not because they believe in something different, but because it's convenient. This isn't rare. This isn't shocking. This is the new normal.

character isn't defined by moments of comfort, it's revealed in moments of pressure. You have to be the same person in every situation, not a shape-shifter who bends to whatever benefits them. If you are kind, be kind without conditions. If you are loyal, be loyal even when power demands betrayal.

Yet, too many people play by different rules. They are loving when no one stops them. They are cold when power commands them. They change because they fear loss, but in doing so, they lose the one thing that truly matters: "TRUTHFULNESS". This is the world we live in. A world where change isn't about growth but about personal gain. A world where people don't ask, "What is right?" but "What is easy?"

But here's the truth. Convenience may protect you for now, but in the end, Honesty is the only thing that stands.

Living like a person you know yourself to be is the best thing!

You are born as a single person, yet to the world, you exist in a thousand different forms. To some, you are an extrovert, full of energy and life. To others, you are quiet, reserved almost a stranger. In one person's life, you are a hero. In another's, you are the villain. Someone sees you as their greatest support, while another remembers you as their biggest betrayal. You are loved deeply in one story and hated fiercely in another. And that's normal.

Because no two people see you the same way. Their judgment is based on their perspective and their experience, not on who you truly are. And perspectives? They change. They always will. But here's what should never change is your core. Above all else, you are human. The world may define you in a thousand ways, but your soul, your essence, your truth ,it should remain untouched. It's not about how people see you. It's about how you see yourself.

People will judge. They always do. Even after you take your last breath, opinions about you will continue to form, twist, and evolve. So why live for them? Why shape yourself according to their shifting perspectives? Live for your own soul. Be who you truly are, not who others want you to be.

If you are strong, that doesn't mean you can't cry. If you need to break down, let yourself. If you feel like shouting, shout. If you choose silence, then be silent. Whatever you do, let it be your choice, not the fear of judgment. People will create versions of you that fit their story. Let them.

But you? You be the character you love. You be the real you. That's the only role that matters.

Maybe endless things give timeless joy!

Life looks very different at every stage, and it's easy to see how the world has mapped out the journey for us. As a child, life was simple. It was all about play, food, and rest. In school, we learned that life is about excelling, moving to the next level. Then, it's about acing public exams to pave the way for college, where we strive for good placements to secure our futures. After that, the cycle continues, work hard in your job to climb the corporate ladder. Then, get married, raise children, and watch them do the same: study, get placed in a good company, marry, and then start the cycle again.

It sounds so easy when you lay it out like this. It sounds simple. But it's not. We like to think that we control our lives, that we can live life on our terms. But society, with its unspoken rules and expectations, often doesn't give us that freedom. For most, it's a rare privilege to live life as they want. A privileged few, one out of a thousand maybe, get to live the life they dream of. For the rest of us? We're caught in the cycle.

After college, we must work. It doesn't matter if you're a man or a woman work is the expectation. You work hard, grind for promotions, and live for the next step in the chain. But here's the hard truth, you are a slave. Not to one person but to the whole system, to the society that dictates the path. You may rise in the ranks, you may get what you want, but you are still bound by the cycle. This is life. It runs on the same tracks. If you question it, it won't change. If you blame the system, nothing will be different. It will keep running the same way it always has. We can't escape it, but we can find ways to make ourselves happy within it. That is the only thing we can control ,our own happiness.

So, yes, the cycle repeats. But maybe, just maybe, you can find joy in your own corner of it. Because in the end, that's the only freedom we truly have.

The hardest Feeling is the first step of healing!

Being emotional does not mean you are incapable. Emotions are a natural part of human experience ,they reflect what we carry within, not how strong we are on the outside. Expressing those emotions, even through tears, should never be mistaken for a lack of resilience.

There may be moments when you feel the need to cry , let it happen. Suppressing your feelings often does more harm than good. Releasing them through tears can bring clarity, peace, and strength. It's not about being fragile; it's about being honest with yourself.

When someone equates crying with weakness, it often comes from a limited understanding of emotional depth. They see only the surface, unaware of the silent battles you have fought before reaching that point. Not everyone will understand and that is alright. Growth takes time, and not everyone is in the same place.

Tears do not diminish your ability to face life. In fact, people who allow themselves to feel deeply are often the ones who handle situations with greater awareness. They do not just react , they reflect. They acknowledge their pain, process it, and move forward with intention.

You do not have to justify your emotions to anyone. And you certainly don't need to suppress them to be seen as strong. True strength lies in embracing your emotions without shame in allowing yourself to feel, and still choosing to move forward with grace.

But make sure emotions are under your control. It could be happiness or sorrow!

But one day, everything changes the way you wanted your life to be!!

You have reached the end.

But some things have been speaking to you from the very beginning.

Every page whispered a part of this.

Every section carried a piece of the truth.

Now, here is what those first lines were gently building toward:

"Your courage, your strength, your wisdom embrace life's lesson! Just celebrate

Pray with purpose.

Love even when the rhythm is quiet.

The moments you are living may be the hardest,

But one day, everything changes the way you wanted your life to be."

Sometimes, the loudest secrets

are the ones hidden in plain sight.

Now that you have heard it,

carry it with you.

Because this one...

It was always meant for you!

Loud Secrets